King David & Akavish the Spider

By Sylvia Rouss

Illustrated by Ari Binus

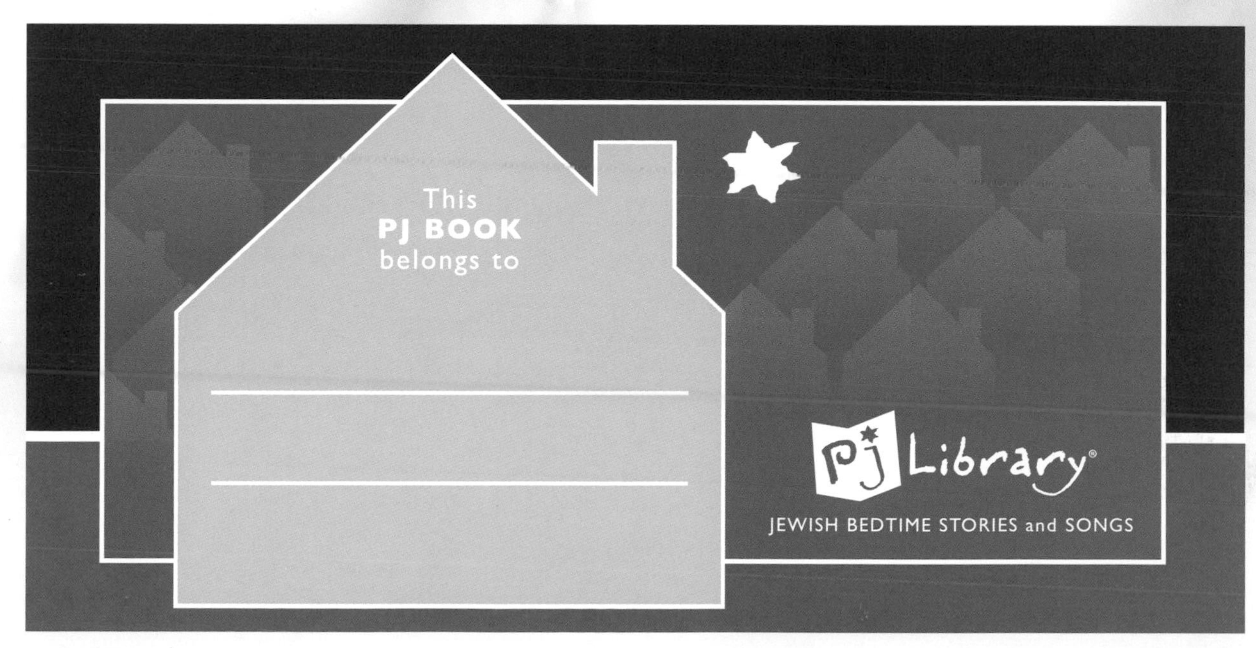

Apples & Honey Press
An imprint of Behrman House and Gefen Publishing House
Behrman House, 11 Edison Place, Springfield, New Jersey 07081
Gefen Publishing House Ltd., 6 Hatzvi Street, Jerusalem 94386, Israel
www.applesandhoneypress.com

ISBN 978-1-68115-504-3

Library of Congress Control Number: 2014941119

Design by Talya Shachar-Albocher
Printed in Israel
1 3 5 7 9 8 6 4 2

071511K1/B0614/A7

A light breeze blew over the hills of Judea as David, a young shepherd boy, watched his sheep grazing. Suddenly his stomach growled.

"I guess I'm hungry too."

David smiled, heading over to the shade of a nearby tree.

Eating his bread and cheese, David looked at King Saul's palace in the distance and wondered what it would be like to live there.

As he wiped the last crumb from his mouth, he noticed a spider web stretched between the branches of the tree.

That web is a perfect target for me to practice my aim! he thought.

He took the sling he used to frighten away wild animals and hurled a small stone at the web. David reloaded his sling and prepared to fling another stone when he heard a small voice say:

“Please stop!”

"Why should I stop?" said David out loud. "It's just a web!"

"It may be just a web to you, but it's my home," said a little spider, dangling from the torn web.

"I'm sorry, Akavish," gulped David, using the Hebrew word for spider. "Can I help you rebuild it?"

“Are you as good at spinning as you are with that sling?” asked the spider.

David shook his head. “No, I’m afraid not,” he answered.

“Then just leave me to my work and promise me that you won’t disturb my web when I’m done.”

David nodded and began playing a tune on his lyre, the small stringed instrument he loved. He watched Akavish move back and forth, weaving in time to the music. "Wow! I never knew how much work goes into building a web."

Just as the sun
began to set,
the little spider
finished.

"It's too dark to head home now," yawned David. "But this cave will be a perfect shelter for me and my sheep. Good night, Akavish."

"Good night, shepherd boy. I enjoyed your music," replied Akavish.

"You may call me David."

"Good night, David," Akavish said softly.

During the night, the wind howled. David felt snug and warm inside the cave with his sheep gathered around him. Then he remembered the little spider.

"Oh, no! I'd better make sure that Akavish is all right."

When David peered out of the cave, he saw Akavish clinging to his torn web.

Suddenly the web broke away from the tree! David gently caught the little spider and carried him into the warm cave.

"Thank you, David," said Akavish. "You saved my life! Maybe one day I will save yours." David smiled, thinking, *How could a tiny little spider ever help me?*

As David grew older, he became an expert with the sling.
He not only used it to protect his sheep from bears and lions,
but against King Saul's enemies too.

The king liked the brave young man. He invited him to live in the palace, where David became good friends with King Saul's son, Jonathan. David often played his lyre for the king and his son, who both loved his music as Akavish did so long ago. At first, King Saul was glad that everyone liked David.

But soon he
became jealous...

One morning, Jonathan heard his father shouting, "The people like David better than me! My own son spends all his time with David! This boy wants to take my place as King. Find him and arrest him at once!"

Jonathan hurried to tell David about the king's plan. "Run into the hills and hide!"

David ran as fast
as he could.

He hid behind bushes,
rocks and trees.

Every time the soldiers
came near, he would find
another hiding place.

Soon he was in the very spot where he had watched his sheep as a boy.

King Saul's soldiers were not far behind.

David dashed inside the cave he once used for shelter. He was so tired of running and although very frightened...

...David closed his eyes
and fell fast asleep.

A loud voice woke David.
It was a soldier shouting.
"Look, there's a cave...
Could he be hiding in there?"
David held his breath as
running feet headed his way.

Suddenly they stopped.

David heard another soldier exclaim, “No! See that web covering the entrance of the cave? It would be broken if David were inside!”

The soldiers hurried away.

When they’d left, David looked up and saw Akavish dangling from the roof of the cave.

“You saved my life long ago,” the spider said. “And I told you that one day I’d save yours!”

David looked with wonder at the web covering the entrance of the cave and remembered how sure he was that the little spider could never help him.

“I see now that strength and might don’t always save the day. Thank you, Akavish!”

David never forgot Akavish.
Years later, when he became King,
David always remembered that small
acts of kindness can make a difference
in great and surprising ways.

Find out Akavish's secret song at
gefenpublishing.com/akavish